Anna and the Letter **A**

Alphabet Friends

by Cynthia Klingel and Robert B. Noyed

The Child's World

The Child's World

**Published in the United States of America
by The Child's World®**
P.O. Box 326
Chanhassen, MN 55317-0326
800-599-READ
www.childsworld.com

The Child's World®: Mary Berendes, Publishing Director

Editorial Directions, Inc.: E. Russell Primm, Editorial
Director; Emily Dolbear, Line Editor; Ruth Martin,
Editorial Assistant; Linda S. Koutris, Photo Researcher
and Selector

Photographs ©: Norbert Schaefer/Corbis: Cover & 11;
Tom Stewart/Corbis: 12; John Bartholomew/Corbis:
15; Martin Harvey; Gallo Images/Corbis: 16; Jack
Stein Grove/PhotoEdit: 19; Kelly/Mooney Photo-
graphy/Corbis: 20.

Library of Congress Cataloging-in-Publication Data
Klingel, Cynthia Fitterer.
  Anna and the letter A / by Cynthia Klingel and
Robert B. Noyed.
     p. cm. – (Alphabet readers)
Summary: A simple story about activities of Anna and
her friend Angelica introduces the letter "a".
Includes bibliographical references (p.) and index.
  ISBN 1-59296-091-X (alk. paper)
  [1. Apples—Fiction. 2. Parks—Fiction. 3. Alphabet.] I.
Noyed, Robert B. II. Title. III Series.
PZ7.K6798An 2003
[E]—dc21
                                          2003006489

Note to parents and educators:
The first skill children acquire before becoming successful readers is individual letter recognition. The Alphabet Friends series has been created with the needs of young learners in mind. Each engaging book begins by showing the difference between the capital letter and the lowercase letter. In each of the books on the vowels and the consonants c and g, children are introduced to the different sounds that the letter can make. Finally, children see that the letters can be found at the beginning of a word, in the middle of a word, and in most cases, at the end of a word.

Following the introduction, children meet their Alphabet Friends. The friend in each story encounters many words that include the featured letter of that book. Each noun that begins with the title letter is highlighted in red with the initial letter of the word in bold. Above the word is a rebus drawing that establishes a strong picture cue.

At the end of each book, we have included three words lists. Can your young learners find all the words in each book with the title letter in them?

Let's learn about the letter **A.**

The letter **A** can look like this: **A.**

The letter **A** can also look like this: **a.**

The letter **a** makes two different sounds.

One sound is the long sound,

like in the word ape.

ape

The other sound is the short sound,

like in the word apple.

apple

The letter **a** can be at the beginning of a word, like animals.

animals

The letter **a** can be in the middle of a word, like cat.

c**a**t

The letter **a** can be at the
end of a word, like banana.

banan**a**

Anna loves to eat **a**pples. There are

apple trees at the park. She goes to the

park with her friend **A**ngelica. They

play by the **a**pple trees.

 Apples fall all around them. Anna and

 Angelica pick apples off the ground.

 They eat the apples and play around

the tree with their friends. They are at

the park all day.

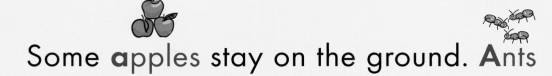

Some **a**pples stay on the ground. **A**nts

crawl on these **a**pples. **A**nts like to eat

apples. **A**nna and **A**ngelica do not

eat any **a**pples with **a**nts on them.

There is a zoo at the park. There are

animals in the zoo. **A**nna likes to see

the **a**pe. The name of the **a**pe is **A**ndy.

Anna asks the zookeeper about the

ape. Anna asks if the ape likes apples.

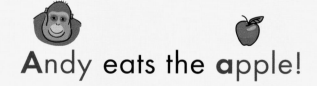

She tosses an apple to Andy the ape.

Andy eats the apple!

Anna and **A**ngelica had a great

day at the park. They ate **a**pples

and saw **a**nimals. They learned

many **A** words.

Fun Facts

 Did you know that most kinds of **a**nimals are less than one inch (2.5 centimeters) long? About half of all **a**nimals are insects. The blue whale is the largest **a**nimal on earth. It can grow to be as big as 100 feet (30 meters) long!

 There are about 10,000 different kinds of **a**nts. Most kinds of **a**nts are brown and black, but some are yellow, green, blue, or purple. **A**nts live in every part of the world except where it is very cold.

 There are five main kinds of **a**pes: bonobos, chimpanzees, gibbons, gorillas, and orangutans. Andy is an orangutan. The name orangutan means "man of the jungle."

 Did you know that the **a**pple is one of the most popular fruits? There are hundreds of kinds of **a**pples. They come in many shapes, sizes, and colors. China grows more **a**pples than any other country.

To Read More

About the Letter A

Ehlert, Lois. *Eating the Alphabet: Fruits & Vegetables from A to Z.* New York: Harcourt Brace, 1996.

Flanagan, Alice K. *Cats: The Sound of Short A.* Chanhassen, Minn.: The Child's World, 2000.

Flanagan, Alice K. *Play Day: The Sound of Long A.* Chanhassen, Minn.: The Child's World, 2000.

About Ants

Cole, Joanna. *Magic School Bus Gets Ants in Its Pants: A Book about Ants.* New York: Scholastic, 1996.

Dorros, Arthur. *Ant Cities.* New York: HarperCollins Children's Books, 1987.

About Apes

Patterson, Francine. *Koko Love!: Conversations with a Talking Gorilla.* New York: Penguin Putnam Books for Young Readers, 1999.

Sourd, Christine. *The Orangutan.* Watertown, Mass.: Charlesbridge Publishing, 2001.

About Apples

Gibbons, Gail. *Apples.* New York: Holiday House, 2000.

Maestro, Betsy C. *How Do Apples Grow?* New York: HarperCollins Children's Books, 1999.

Words with A

Words with A at the Beginning

a
about
all
also
an
and
Andy
Angelica
animals
Anna
ants
any
ape
apple
apples
are
around
asks
at
ate

Words with A in the Middle

animals
banana
can
cat
crawl
day
eat
eats
fall
great
had
learn
learned
makes
many
name
park
play
saw
stay

Words with A at the End

Angelica
Anna
banana

About the Authors

Cynthia Klingel has worked as a high school English teacher and an elementary teacher. She is currently the curriculum director for a Minnesota school district. Cynthia Klingel lives with her family in Mankato, Minnesota.

Robert B. Noyed started his career as a newspaper reporter. Since then, he has worked in communications and public relations for a Minnesota school district for more than fourteen years. Robert B. Noyed lives with his family in Brooklyn Center, Minnesota.